What the Little Fir Tree Wore to the Christmas Party

For

Édouard,

Miyoko & Einar,

and

Nanette

What the Little Fir Tree Wore to the Christmas Party

SATOMI ICHIKAWA

PHILOMEL BOOKS

★t is almost Christmas, and at the edge of the forest, the
fir trees begin to stir their branches with excitement.
None of the trees has been to a Christmas party before, but
they are excited to go.

The biggest tree bows down toward her friends. "What are you going to wear to the party?" she whispers eagerly. "Oh, I was just trying to decide!" says a smaller, bright green tree. "We've waited for so long—it has to be perfect!" All the trees begin to talk at once about what they will wear to the party. In the shadows of the giant trees, a very small tree is listening. Nobody notices her.

"I'm going to wear a dress of beautiful flowers," exclaims a round, bushy tree.

"No, no!" snaps the biggest. "Christmas is not a celebration of spring, you know."

The round tree shrugs softly. The truth is, since none of the trees has been to a Christmas party before, each can only imagine what a Christmas tree should look like.

"I've heard that Christmas is a celebration of light,"
declares a triangle-shaped tree. "That's why I want to wear a
dress with lights, like a golden sunset! I'm tired of
always wearing green."
"I've always dreamed of wearing a rainbow
dress," says a tall, graceful tree.
The tiny tree in the shadows
is still listening.

"As for me," says the biggest tree, "I want to dress in a thousand twinkling stars and stand in the middle of the grandest avenue in all the world!"

The other trees stand back, dazzled by the thought of the biggest tree's dream.

The little one watches, too. She is beginning to have an idea about what she will wear to the party, but no one pays her any attention.

"Why don't they ask me?" she thinks sadly.

The days pass, and Christmas is getting closer. One morning, a scratching, roaring noise fills the forest. The littlest tree trembles with fear from her roots to the tips of her needles.

The terrible noise stops and starts up again, coming closer and closer. The little fir shakes so hard, she loses many of her needles. "What is happening?" she cries.

When it is finally quiet again, the tiny tree looks up. The sky is wide open. "Where are all the others? Where did everyone go?" she wonders in alarm. She turns just in time to see a truck disappearing into the distance, the rest of the trees in the back of it. "They have left without me," she cries.

"Wait! Don't leave me here!" she calls. "I want to go to the party, too!" She tries with all her strength to follow, but she can't move from her place in the forest.

"Now I am all alone." She bows her head.
"But you are not alone," a low voice whispers on the wind.

The littlest tree notices an old, bare tree standing nearby.

"Oh, you didn't go to the party, either," the little tree sighs with relief.

The kindly old tree bends down. "What is your Christmas dream, little one?" he asks.

The little fir is so happy to find someone who will listen to her! "I want to wear a long dress—all in white—like a veil of moon," she says. Then her branches sink. "But it's too late now. Everyone's gone to the party, and I am still here.

"But what about you?" asks the little tree. "Did you have a Christmas dream?"

The crooked tree smiles sadly. "No, I am too old," he says.

"No, you're not!" exclaims the little tree. "Dreams are for you, too."

The two trees spend the next few days sharing their dreams and stories about Christmas. Before they know it, it is Christmas morning. When the little fir wakes up, she sees a white dress falling from the sky, delicately covering her branches. She stares in wonder as it gently dresses her.

When the sun shines, her white dress sparkles like thousands of lights. "Oh," says the old tree. "How beautiful you are!"

"But look at yourself! You are beautiful, too!" the tiny
tree says. Birds of all colors have perched on the branches
of the crooked old tree. They sing songs that fill the air—
wonderful, happy songs that make the trees think of rain-
bows and starlight and beautiful springtime flowers.

"What a wonderful Christmas gift!" the little tree marvels.

"And we will have our own party," says the old tree to his little friend.

And in this way they spend the most wonderful Christmas together.

PATRICIA LEE GAUCH, EDITOR

With special thanks to Courtenay Lewis

PHILOMEL BOOKS,
a division of Penguin Putnam Books for Young Readers,
345 Hudson Street, New York, NY 10014. Philomel Books,
Reg. U.S. Pat. & Tm. Off. Published simultaneously in Canada.
First published in France in 1999 by l'école des loisirs, Paris.
Printed in Hong Kong by South China Printing Co. (1988) Ltd.
Designed by Semadar Megged.
Text set in 17-point Weiss.
The art was done in watercolor.
Library of Congress Cataloging-in-Publication Data

ISBN 0-399-23746-1
1 3 5 7 9 10 8 6 4 2
First American Edition